TESSA KRAILING

The Petsitters Club

5. Scruncher Goes Wandering

Illustrated by Jan Lewis

BARRON'S

First edition for the United States, Canada, and the Philippines published by Barron's Educational Series, Inc., 1998.

Text Copyright © Tessa Krailing, 1997
Illustrations Copyright © Jan Lewis, 1997

First published in Great Britain in 1997 by Scholastic Children's Books, Commonwealth House, 1-19 New Oxford Street, London WC1A 1NU, UK
A division of Scholastic Ltd

Barron's Educational Series, Inc.
250 Wireless Boulevard
Hauppauge, New York 11788
http://www.barronseduc.com

ISBN 0-7641-0574-4
Library of Congress Catalog Card No. 97-38853

Library of Congress Cataloging-in-Publication Data

Krailing, Tessa, 1935-
    The Petsitters Club. 5, Scruncher goes wandering / Tessa Krailing.—1st ed.
        p. cm.
    Summary: The Petsitters agree to look after the principal's potbellied pig at the school fair, but the job turns out to be more complicated than they had anticipated.
    ISBN 0-7641-0574-4
    [1. Clubs—Fiction. 2. Potbellied pig—Fiction. 3. Pigs—Fiction. 4. Fairs—Fiction.] I. Title.
PZ7.K85855Sc   1998
[Fic]—dc21   97-38853
                                                                CIP
                                                                 AC

Printed in the United States of America
9 8 7 6 5 4 3 2 1

Chapter 1

A Really Important Job

Sam called the other Petsitters together. "Mr. Grantham wants to see us," she told them.

Matthew turned pale. "Why? What have we done wrong?"

"No idea," said Sam. "But we've got to go to his office right away."

Mr. Grantham was their principal—and if Mr. Grantham sent for you it usually meant *big trouble*.

Jovan looked worried. "Someone must have complained about us. Maybe it was that lady whose cat piddled on the carpet while we were watching it."

"Or it could have been that old man with the ferrets," said Matthew. "When I told him that one of them bit me, he said I was making a fuss about nothing."

Sam felt worried, too, but she was determined not to show it. She said briskly, "Well, it's no use hanging around worrying about it. Let's go and find out."

"What about Katie?" asked Matthew. "Do you think he wants to see her, too?"

Matthew's younger sister Katie was also a member of the Petsitters Club. Her job was to look after the creepy-crawlies.

"You'd better go and get her,

Matthew," said Sam.

Matthew went into the playground. He returned with a cross-looking Katie.

"I was busy feeding the ants," she

grumbled. "What does silly old Mr. Grantham want anyway?"

"Sssh!" hissed Jovan. "He might hear you."

"I don't care if he does." Katie looked rebellious.

Sam took a deep breath and knocked

on Mr. Grantham's door. All four Petsitters stood shaking in their sneakers.

"Come in, come in." Mr. Grantham had a very deep voice.

They filed in and stood in front of his desk, four pairs of eyes fixed on his face. It was rather a stern face, although it

could look quite kind when he smiled.

"Ah, the Petsitters," he said. "Just the people I wanted to see. Now, you know that next Saturday will be the School Fair?"

Four heads nodded.

"Well, I have a little job for you, if you're interested."

"A job?" echoed four voices. This wasn't at all what they had expected.

"Yes." He turned rather pink, which

was unusual for Mr. Grantham. "You may or may not know that I have, er, a pet pig."

"A *pig?*" echoed the same four voices.

"Yes, a miniature pot-bellied pig. She's called—er . . ." Mr. Grantham turned even pinker. "Scruncher."

The four Petsitters stared at him. Their principal owned a pet pig called Scruncher! They could hardly believe it.

Mr. Grantham went on, "My wife thought it might be a good idea to bring her along to the Fair and let people try to guess her weight."

"Will there be a prize?" asked Sam.

"Yes, five dollars for the person who guesses the closest." Mr. Grantham smiled, which made him look much less stern. "I think they'll find it difficult. She's heavier than she looks. But of course Mrs. Grantham and I will have a lot of other things to do that day so we'd like the Petsitters to watch her. Will you do it?"

Before the others had a chance to speak, Katie began, "Sorry, but I . . ."

Matthew kicked her ankle. "Yes, sir. We'll do it."

"It's a good thing there are four of you," said Mr. Grantham. "You'll need one person to write down people's guesses while the others keep an eye on Scruncher."

"Will we get points for it?" asked Sam.

"Points? Oh, for the community

service project." Mr. Grantham glanced at the chart on his wall, which showed how many points had been earned so far by the children competing for the school's community service trophy. In the lead, was a group who went around visiting the elderly. Second came two girls who did shopping for the housebound. The Petsitters were in third place. "Yes, of course you'll get points. Double, if you do a good job of it."

"*Double!*" echoed the three older

Petsitters, delighted.

The youngest, Katie, said, "But I can't."

Matthew stomped on her toe. "Don't worry, sir. We'll watch Scruncher. She'll be safe with us."

Mr. Grantham looked pleased. "Be waiting in the parking lot, one-thirty sharp. We want to have the stall set up

and ready before the Fair starts
promptly at two o'clock. You may go."

The Petsitters filed out of his office.

Outside in the corridor, Matthew

said, "Imagine Mr. Grantham wanting to use our petsitting service!"

Sam said seriously, "You realize this is the most important job we've ever had? We'd better not mess it up, whatever we do. We must *all* be there, *all* the time, to keep on eye on Scruncher."

"You can count me out," said Katie, rubbing her ankle and toe. "I keep trying to tell you, my pet cockroach Archie is running in the cockroach race. I'll be much too busy to watch a pig."

"You can count me out, too," said Jovan. "I don't like pigs."

"Oh, Jo!" said Sam. "This is only a

15

miniature pig. She'll be tiny, like a little puppy."

Jovan looked unconvinced. "You heard what Mr. Grantham said. She's heavier than she looks. Anyway, pigs smell and they go *oink*. I don't like them."

Sam sighed. "All right, you can be in charge of writing down people's guesses. Matthew and I will watch the pig and Katie will have to come and help as soon as her cockroach race is over. This job is worth double points, remember? We've got to get it right."

Chapter 2

The Morning of the Fair

On the morning of the Fair, Sam said, "I'm feeling nervous."

"Mmm?" said Dad, who was drawing a cartoon animal on his sketch pad.

"We've got to watch this pig, you see. And it's a very special pig."

"Mmm?" He added two ears and a tail.

"It belongs to Mr. Grantham."

"Ah." Dad stopped drawing and looked up. "Tell me again. I wasn't listening well."

Sam sighed. Dad never listened well when he was working. "Mr. Grantham's asked the Petsitters to watch his pet pig," she explained. "He's bringing it to the Fair so that people can try to guess its weight. It's called Scruncher."

18

"Why are you nervous?"

"Dad, this is the *principal's* pig! If something goes wrong, we could get into *big trouble*." Sam's stomach began to rumble. It often rumbled when she was nervous. She tried to reassure herself. "But of course nothing *will* go wrong. Why should it? What possible trouble could we get into watching a pig?"

A slow smile spread over Dad's face. "No idea," he said. But he added a snout to his cartoon animal and gave it a very mischievous expression.

On the morning of the Fair, Jovan was eating a bowl of sugar puffs. At least, he was *trying* to eat sugar puffs, but he seemed to have lost his appetite.

"Is something the matter?" asked his mother.

Jovan sighed. "We have to watch this pig."

"What sort of a pig?" asked his father, who was Dr. Roy, the veterinarian.

"It's a pet pig. One of those small ones with a big stomach."

"You mean a Vietnamese pot-bellied pig," said Dr. Roy. "Intelligent little creatures. Very attractive when they're small. The trouble is they tend to grow bigger than people expect."

Jovan gulped. "How big?"

"Too big to pick up and carry around as you can when they're babies. People think they can treat them like a dog, taking them out for walks and so on. But a full-grown, pot-bellied pig is quite a responsibility."

In Jovan's imagination Mr. Grantham's pig grew bigger and bigger.

22

"They're very strong," Dr. Roy went on. "If they make up their minds to do something, nothing will stop them."

In Jovan's imagination Mr. Grantham's pig became a giant. A giant hog with an enormous pot-belly and mean little eyes.

23

"Do you know its name?" asked Mrs. Roy.

"He said it was called Scruncher," said Jovan.

Why was it called Scruncher? Because it scrunched people up? Jovan's imaginary pig grew long tusks and came charging out of the bushes like an angry wild boar.

24

"If you take my advice, Jo," said Dr. Roy, "you won't let it out of your sight for an instant."

Jovan made up his mind that he wasn't going near that pig if he could possibly help it. In his imagination, it had just trampled him to death.

On the morning of the Fair, Matthew and Katie were arguing.

"If you want to be a good Petsitter, you should help us with the pig," said Matthew. "Not go off to play with your cockroach."

"I'm *not* playing with him," said Katie indignantly. "I'm *racing* him. And I know he's going to win."

"I wouldn't count on it," said Matthew. "He's a pretty slow mover considering he's got six legs."

"Archie's the fastest cockroach in the world!" Katie protested. "He's a lot faster than Ryan Bates' Lightning."

"*Lightning!*" Matthew laughed. "Anyway, how can you race two cockroaches? They'll fight each other."

"No they won't. Ryan's dad has made a special racetrack with barriers to keep them apart. We put our roaches in one end and then coax them along with a bit of banana. Archie loves bananas."

Matthew yawned. "Sounds pretty boring to me. Who wants to watch a couple of insects crawling after a banana?"

"Lots of people," said Katie obstinately. "You'll see."

"You'd be far better off helping us with the pig," said Matthew, equally obstinate.

Katie knelt down beside the tank where Archie lived with his family. "He doesn't understand," she whispered. "Nobody does. But you're going to win this race, Archie, aren't you?"

She stroked Archie with the tip of her finger. He hissed at her warningly.

"It's all right, dear. Don't be afraid. Look, here's a piece of banana. You love banana, don't you? You'll run fast for a banana. No, you can't have too much now. I want you to stay a little bit hungry for the race."

She stroked Archie again. This time he didn't hiss.

"There, what a brave cockroach you are. Much better than any silly old pig. Anyway, you don't need four people to watch a pig. Sam and Matthew can do it easily on their own. Oh, I can't *wait* for this afternoon!"

Chapter 3

Scruncher

To Sam's relief, all four Petsitters arrived in the parking lot on time.

"I'm not stopping," said Katie, clutching a cardboard box. "I only came because Matthew said you'd throw me out of the Petsitters Club if I didn't."

"I said she had to be here when the principal arrives," Matthew explained.

"He's only letting us watch his pig because he thinks there are four of us. If we're one short, he could change his mind."

At that moment, a green Range Rover entered the parking lot, driven by Mr. Grantham. He turned off the engine and got out. "Hello, Petsitters!" he called. "Come and meet Scruncher."

Cautiously, they approached the Range Rover. Mr. Grantham opened the back and let down a ramp. First to appear was his wife, holding a long leash.

"Come on, Scruncher." She gave the leash a gentle tug. "Don't be shy."

Nothing happened.

Mrs. Grantham tugged harder on the leash.

Still nothing happened. Mrs. Grantham tugged even harder.

"Here, let me try," said Mr. Grantham impatiently. He grabbed the leash from his wife. "Come on, Scruncher. Stop being an obstinate little pig!"

He tugged again and a small black pig shot down the ramp. Taken by surprise, Mr. Grantham fell over backwards, still clutching the leash. His wife burst out laughing.

"Oh!" Sam stared down at the pig. "Isn't she pretty?"

"She's not as big as I thought she'd be," said Jovan, sounding relieved.

"You can see why she's called pot-bellied," said Katie. "She has a very fat stomach."

"And very short legs," said Matthew.

Mrs. Grantham was still laughing at her husband. "Oh George, you do look funny. And in your best suit, too!"

"Could somebody help me up, please?" said Mr. Grantham frostily.

His wife handed the leash to Sam and helped her husband to his feet. He brushed himself off and glared at Scruncher, who was looking around the lot with interest.

"As you can see, she's quite a handful," he said. "Do you think you'll be able to watch her, Petsitters?"

"Oh, yes!" Sam bent down to pat Scruncher's sleek, black back. "You don't have to worry, sir. We'll take care of her."

Jovan cleared his throat. "Why is she called Scruncher?" he asked.

"I named her that as soon as I saw her," said Mrs. Grantham. "It's because she has such a lovely little scrunched-up face."

38

"Oh, I see." Jovan looked as if a great weight had been taken off his mind.

Scruncher began snuffling around Katie's feet. Katie backed away hastily. "What's the matter? What does she want?"

"It's that banana sticking out of your pocket," said Mrs. Grantham. "Scruncher loves bananas."

"Well, she can't have this one," said Katie. "I need it to make Archie run in the cockroach ra—*ow!*" She stopped as Matthew dug his elbow into her ribs.

"Don't worry," said Mrs. Grantham. "We've brought some bananas for you to give Scruncher if she gets bored. Now let's go and find the stall we set up for her this morning."

They found the stall behind the snack tent, under the trees. It was really just a square patch of grass surrounded by a wire fence. Inside was some hay, a table and chair, and a sign saying *Guess My Weight*.

"It's a bit tucked away," Sam said doubtfully. "Wouldn't it be better if we were near the castle bounce or the ice-cream truck?"

"We chose this place because it's in the shade," Mr. Grantham explained. "And because it's quiet. Scruncher might get frightened if she was in a busy place with too much noise. Take her inside and see if she likes it."

Sam took Scruncher into the stall. Scruncher snuffled around. When she found the hay, she made little grunting noises of delight and started tossing it into the air.

"You can take off her leash now that she's safe," said Mrs. Grantham. "Who's in charge of writing down people's guesses?"

"I am," said Jovan.

Mrs. Grantham handed him a cash box and a large red notebook. "You charge them 10 cents for each guess. And be sure you get their addresses as well as their names in case they go home before the winner's announced."

"How much *does* she weigh?" asked Matthew, looking curiously at Scruncher.

"Ah, that's secret information," said Mr. Grantham. "Only my wife and I know the answer to that. Now here's the bag of bananas. Don't give her too many at once. And here's her water bowl."

"Be a good girl, Scruncher." Mrs. Grantham gave the pig a final pat. She turned to the Petsitters. "If there's any trouble come and find me at once."

"There won't be any trouble," Sam said confidently. "We're the experts."

Chapter 4

The Fastest Cockroach in the World

"I'm going now," said Katie as soon as Mr. and Mrs. Grantham had gone.

Matthew sighed. "Well, all right. But don't let Mr. Grantham see you or we'll all be in trouble."

"I won't," Katie promised.

"And come right back here when it's over," said Sam.

"I will," Katie promised.

She hurried in the direction of the table she had spotted earlier. The long table with a sign above saying *Grand Cockroach Race*. Ryan Bates was already there with his dad, and he was giving his cockroach Lightning a practice run.

"That's cheating!" she protested.

Ryan looked annoyed. "We're only testing the track. My dad wants to see if it works well."

Katie glared at him. "I bet you've been giving Lightning practice runs all week. You've been training him, that's what you've been doing!"

"Now, now," said Mr. Bates, "let's not have any arguing. Katie can give her cockroach a practice run as well. That's only fair."

"No, thanks," said Katie. "I don't want him to get tired before the race.

48

Anyway, Archie doesn't need a practice run. He's the fastest cockroach in the world."

"No, he's not," said Ryan.

"Yes, he is."

"No, he's—"

"That's enough!" said Mr. Bates, who was beginning to look rather annoyed. "We'll soon find out which is the fastest when they start racing. It's a pity there's only two of them, but never mind."

"Can we have the race now, please?" Katie asked. "Archie doesn't like being shut up in this box. He keeps hissing."

"We can't have it before the Fair's been officially opened," said Mr. Bates. "I've asked Mr. Grantham to announce it so that people come and watch."

At that moment, a loud screeching noise came from the loudspeaker. Then Mr. Grantham's voice boomed out. "Ladies and gentlemen, I have pleasure in declaring our Fair is now open! We

have a number of interesting things for you to do and see today. There's a cake stall, a castle bounce, and a *Guess My Weight* competition, featuring Scruncher the pig. You'll find that behind the snack tent. And in addition to the children's races, we have a cockroach race, which I'm told will be very exciting."

Katie opened the lid of the box. She whispered to Archie, "Don't be nervous, dear. You'll win easily. I know you will. Just follow the banana."

"Okay, get your cockroaches ready," said Mr. Bates. "Mr. Grantham has kindly agreed to start the race for us."

"Mr. *Grantham?*" said Katie, horrified.

"Yes, he'll be here soon."

Oh no! Matthew had said that if Mr. Grantham saw her, they'd all be in trouble. What was she going to do?

Chapter 5

Wandering

Sam, Matthew, and Jovan were getting bored. Hardly anyone had come near their stall and only one person had actually tried to guess Scruncher's weight, a woman who wrote ten pounds in Jovan's book.

Jovan stared down at what she had written. "Ten pounds! That's the same as a bag of potatoes. I bet Scruncher weighs a lot more than that."

"How much more?" challenged Matthew.

Jovan shrugged. "Forty-five pounds at least."

"Go on, then," said Sam. "Write it down in the book."

Jovan wrote it down.

"Now put 10 cents in the box," said Sam. "Otherwise it won't count."

Reluctantly Jovan paid. "Okay, now it's your turn," he said.

Matthew wrote down fifty pounds and Sam put sixty.

"Sixty?" Jovan stared at her. "She can't possibly weigh as much as that!"

"Remember what Mr. Grantham said? She's heavier than she looks."

Matthew gazed at Scruncher's portly figure. "She does have an enormous pot-belly. Maybe I'd better make mine seventy-two . . ."

"Oh, no." Jovan closed the book with a snap. "You can't go changing your mind. If you want to guess again, you'll have to pay another 10 cents."

"No way!" said Matthew.

After a while, Scruncher got fed up with snuffling around the hay. She lay down on her side and closed her eyes.

"She's as bored as we are," said Sam. "I knew Mr. Grantham put this stall in the wrong place. Nobody's ever going to find us here."

"They'll see us when they come to the snack tent," said Matthew.

"It won't be dinnertime for ages yet," Jovan said gloomily.

After a while, Matthew said, "If we walked Scruncher around a bit, I bet lots of people would see her and want to guess her weight."

"Mr. Grantham said she's not used to crowds," Jovan said doubtfully. "She might get frightened."

"We don't need to take her anywhere crowded," said Matthew.

"I don't think it could do any harm," said Sam. "After all, she's used to being taken for walks. That's why she has a harness and a leash."

"I still think we should ask Mr. Grantham's permission," said Jovan.

"All right," said Matthew. "Let's go and find him."

"We'll have to take Scruncher with us," said Sam.

She clipped the leash onto the harness.

Scruncher immediately scrambled to her feet, looking interested.

"There!" said Sam, delighted. "She wants to go for a walk. I knew she would."

"I'll bring the book and the cash box," said Jovan, "in case anyone makes a guess while we're walking around. Matthew, you'd better bring the sign."

"Okay."

The three of them left the stall, Scruncher trotting along beside them. The first person they met was Ben Duke, who sat next to Matthew in class. "About eighty," he said.

"What?" said Matthew.

"Your weight." He pointed to the sign Matthew was carrying. "I'm seventy pounds and you're heavier than I am, so yes, I guess about eighty."

"It's not *my* weight you have to guess," said Matthew. "It's the pig's."

"Then why isn't the pig carrying the sign?" asked Ben, and walked off.

"Hey, wait!" Sam called after him. "Do you know where Mr. Grantham is?"

"Last time I saw him, he was going to start the cockroach race," Ben called back.

"The cockroach race?" Matthew turned pale. "Oh, no! He'll see Katie!"

"Come on," said Sam. "We'd better get over there."

They found such a large crowd around the racetrack that they couldn't get near enough to see what was happening.

"Who'd have thought so many people would want to watch a cockroach race?" said Sam.

"We're still waiting for it to start," said a woman standing beside her. "One of the cockroaches is missing."

Mr. Bates' voice rang out above the hubbub. "I'm sorry, ladies and gentlemen, but we can't possibly have a race with only one cockroach. Has anyone seen Katie White? She seems to have disappeared and we can't start without her."

"Katie White? Where's Katie White?" everyone murmured.

Matthew groaned. "I'd better go and find out what's happened."

"I'll come with you." Sam turned to Jovan. "You'll have to look after Scruncher. I can't take her into this crowd."

She thrust the leash at him. At the same time, Matthew handed him the *Guess My Weight* sign, saying, "Here, hold this for me." Then they both disappeared, leaving Jovan with the book, and the cash box, and the sign, and Scruncher's leash.

63

"Oh, no!" Jovan groaned, trying to hold all of them at once. "I *knew* something like this would happen!"

At that moment Ben Duke came along again. "Hi, Jo!" he said. "So now it's *your* weight we have to guess, is it?"

"Ha, ha!" said Jovan sarcastically. "That's the second time you've cracked that joke, and it wasn't even funny the first time."

"It's funny this time," said Ben with a grin, "because you don't have a pig."

"Yes I have!"

"Where is it, then?"

Jovan looked down. He had the book and the box and the sign all right, but he didn't have the leash. And no leash meant no harness. And no harness meant . . .

No Scruncher!

Chapter 6

Tug-of-Banana

Katie, still clutching her cardboard box, was hiding under the Fruit and Vegetable Stand. Outside she could hear people calling her name. "Katie White? Has anyone seen Katie White?" and she wished they'd stop. By now everyone must know that it was her cockroach that was missing, including

Mr. Grantham. If only Ryan's dad hadn't asked him to start the race!

She lifted the lid of the box. "Archie, are you all right?"

Archie hissed at her.

"Don't worry, dear," she reassured him. "We're safe. No one will think of looking for us here."

The Fruit and Vegetable Stand was covered by a red-and-white checked tablecloth that came nearly to the ground. It was like being in a tent. Peering out from underneath, Katie could see feet moving about and hear muffled voices:

"I'll have a pound of tomatoes, please, and a head of lettuce. Oh, and those apples look nice. I'll have a pound of them, too."

She whispered to Archie, "As soon as all the fuss dies down, we'll make a run for it."

Then she heard Matthew's voice.

"Katie? Katie, where are you?"

Cautiously Katie lifted the edge of the tablecloth. Yes, those were definitely Matthew's sneakers. She recognized them from the muddy toes. If she could just reach out and give his jeans a tug . . . .

But then she heard another voice. A deep, booming voice that unmistakably belonged to Mr. Grantham.

"Matthew White, what are you doing here?" A pair of large black shoes joined Matthew's sneakers. "And where's Scruncher?"

"Oh, hello, sir." Matthew sounded nervous. "Scruncher's with Jo. We, er, decided to take her for a walk."

"*For a walk?*"

"She was getting bored, sir. And nobody was coming to guess her weight, so we thought . . . ."

"Where's Jovan now?"

"Over there somewhere."

"Go and find him right away." Mr. Grantham sounded stern. "And take Scruncher back to her stall. As soon as I've started this cockroach race, I will come and make sure she's all right."

"Yes, sir. Sorry, sir."

Matthew's sneakers disappeared and so did the large black shoes.

Katie shivered. Any minute now Mr. Grantham would be arriving at the racetrack.

Then she heard another familiar voice.

"Hello, Jo," said Sam. "What are you doing here?"

Cautiously Katie lifted a corner of the tablecloth. She could see Sam's feet and Jovan's feet not far away. If she could only just reach . . .

"I've lost Scruncher," said Jovan.

"*What?* You can't have!"

"It happened when you gave me the leash and Matthew gave me the sign. I couldn't hold everything at once, so I, er, must have dropped the leash."

"Oh, no!" groaned Sam. "Come on, we've got to find her."

Their feet disappeared before Katie had a chance to reach out far enough. Disappointed, she let the tablecloth drop.

At the same moment she heard an odd snuffling noise behind her. Something had joined her under the table. Oh, please, not a dog! If the owner came looking for it they'd be sure to find her. She felt something nudge against her feet. Without turning around, she muttered, "Go away, dog! Leave me alone!"

But the snuffling only grew louder. She felt a sharp tug at her jeans pocket. Angrily she turned around, and found herself looking straight into the snout of a small black pig.

"Scruncher!" she exclaimed.

Scruncher scrunched up her face. Snuffle, snuffle.

"They're looking for you," Katie told her. "And they're looking for me, too, so we're both in trouble."

Scruncher didn't seem particularly worried by this news. She was far more interested in what was sticking out of Katie's jeans pocket. Snuffle, snuffle, nudge, nudge.

"Hey, what are you doing?" Katie demanded. "Oh, I see. You want the banana. Well, you can't have it. That's Archie's and . . . ."

Too late! Scruncher had already snatched the banana and was running off with it. Still clutching her cardboard box, Katie crawled after her.

"Give it back, you greedy pig!"

She pounced on Scruncher, but Scruncher gave a little squeal and wriggled free. Katie pounced again, and managed to grab one end of the banana. But Scruncher wouldn't let go.

Katie tugged. Scruncher tugged.

Katie tugged harder. Scruncher tugged harder. It was like a tug-of-war, except it was a tug-of-banana.

Katie tugged harder still. Scruncher tugged harder still, and this time she managed to pull the banana free!

Taken by surprise, Katie fell back against the leg of the trestle table. The leg began to wobble. The whole table began to wobble. Slowly it tipped sideways, and everything on it slid to the ground.

Someone screamed. Potatoes, apples, pears, and cauliflowers rolled everywhere. Tomatoes fell SPLAT! onto the ground. A large head of lettuce landed on Katie's head as she crawled out from under the tablecloth. To her horror, she saw Scruncher disappearing into the crowd with Archie's banana sticking out of her mouth.

"Stop that pig!" yelled Katie.

Chapter 7

A Fun Day Out

Exhausted, Sam and Jovan stopped by the snack tent. "Scruncher can't have gone far," said Sam. "She only has little legs."

Matthew came rushing up. "There you are!" he exclaimed. "I just met Mr. Grantham and told him we'd taken Scruncher for a walk. He said we had to take her straight back to her stall."

"We can't," Sam said miserably. "We've lost her."

"She ran off," Jovan explained. "We've been looking for her everywhere."

Matthew groaned. "He will be *furious!*"

"He'll be more than furious," Sam said. "He'll probably explode."

They looked helplessly at each other.

At that moment, two women stopped and stared at the sign Jovan was still holding. "Is it that dear little pig's weight we're supposed to be guessing?" one of them asked. "If so, I'd like to guess at forty-four pounds."

"Oh, no. I'd say nearer fifty," said the other.

Jovan said, "But, but how can you make a guess when you haven't seen her?"

"We saw her just a minute ago," said the first woman. "She's in that stall behind the snack tent. Should we write it in the book?"

She took the book out of Jovan's hand and started writing.

"Did you say, in the *stall?*" asked Sam.

"That's right. All by herself, fast asleep." She handed the book to her friend.

The three Petsitters stared at each other. Could it be true?

The first woman handed the book back to Jovan. "There. How much do we owe you?"

"Er, that'll be 20 cents, please," said Jovan.

The two women paid and disappeared into the snack tent.

The Petsitters sped around the back to the stall. Sure enough, Scruncher was asleep in the hay with something yellow sticking out of her mouth.

"She must have come back all by herself," said Sam.

"How did she find the way?" asked Matthew.

"My dad told me that pigs were intelligent," said Jovan.

"She's more than just intelligent," said Sam. "She's *brilliant!*"

Katie came rushing up. "So there she is! And oh, she's eaten nearly all of Archie's banana, the greedy little pig!"

Matthew glared at his sister. "Where have you been? I've looked for you everywhere."

"I hid under the Fruit and Vegetable Stand," Katie told him. "And then Scruncher came to join me and that's when she . . . ."

"Sssh!" he warned. "Here's Mr. Grantham."

The principal came over to the stall. "Ah, Katie! It suddenly occurred to me that you might be here. You'd better hurry. You and your cockroach are wanted on the racetrack."

"But, but, sir," Katie stammered, "you said you wanted all four of us to watch Scruncher . . ."

"I didn't mean all four of you had to stay with her *all* the time," he said. "Come on, the sooner we get this race started the better."

Katie didn't move. She just stood there, staring at him.

"What's the matter?" he asked.

"I don't have a banana," she said. "And Archie won't run without one."

"That's easily solved." Mrs. Grantham stepped out from behind the snack tent. "You can have one of Scruncher's."

She took a banana from the bag and handed it to Katie.

"Thanks," said Katie. She hurried off with Mr. Grantham, still clutching her cardboard box.

"Well done, Petsitters," said Mrs. Grantham. "That was a good idea of yours, taking Scruncher for a walk. Look,

you've got quite a line of people waiting to make a guess. They must have seen Scruncher while she was on her travels and came to find the stall."

Sam saw with surprise that she was right, and at the front of the line was Ben Duke. "My guess is seventy-two pounds," he said, putting a dime on the

table. "And this time I'm talking about the pig."

Jovan sat down and started writing in his book.

Sam said to Mrs. Grantham, "You're not angry that we took Scruncher for a walk?"

Mrs. Grantham shook her head. "No, I'm not angry. Although I might have been if you'd lost her."

Sam blushed. "Yes, but even if she'd gotten lost, she'd have found her way back here, wouldn't she? She's a very smart pig."

Mrs. Grantham smiled. "Pretty smart," she agreed. "But not quite smart enough to take off her own leash. Now I must go and watch the cockroach race." She walked away.

Sam and Matthew stared at Scruncher's leash hanging neatly over the chair.

"How do you think it got there?" asked Matthew.

"You know what I think?" said Sam. "I think Mrs. Grantham must have found Scruncher wandering around and brought her back. That's why she was standing so close to the snack tent."

"Do you think she'll tell Mr. Grantham?"

Sam groaned. "Well, if she does, we won't get our double points, that's for sure!"

"Anything happen at the Fair?" asked Dad when Sam got home.

"Plenty!" said Sam.

She told him everything. He listened intently, at the same time drawing on his sketch pad.

When she had finished, he asked, "And did Archie win the cockroach race?"

"No, he wouldn't move an inch, not even when Katie dangled a piece of banana in front of him. She said it was because he felt sick after being jostled around in the cardboard box."

"Who won the *Guess My Weight* competition?" asked Dad.

Sam made a face. "Ben Duke. His guess of seventy-two pounds was exactly right. Matthew was furious because that was what he'd wanted to put and Jovan wouldn't let him change his mind."

"And did you get your double points?"

"Yes! So we guess Mrs. Grantham couldn't have told Mr. Grantham what really happened." Sam looked over her father's shoulder. "What are you drawing?"

He showed her.

The End

Join The Petsitters Club for *more* animal adventures!

1. Jilly the Kid
2. The Cat Burglar
3. Donkey Rescue
4. Snake Alarm!
6. Trixie and the Cyber Pet